This book is given lovingly
to Aria and Zoila, our delightful,
precious grand daughters!
Sept. 2012   Zoila's 2nd Birthday
Aria's birth

We love you adoringly
♡ ♡ Bebe + Papa

You Are a Gift to the World

By Laura Duksta

Illustrated by Dona Turner

sourcebooks
jabberwocky

Praise for *You Are a Gift to the World*

"*I Love You More* has become a family favorite. Now with her second book, *You Are a Gift to the World*, Laura is helping to expand the conversation of love. Her message is a gift to our children, our families and our planet. With much XOXO."

—Lyss Stern founder of Divalysscious Moms, www.divamoms.com

"Laura writes for the children of *our* world from a deep place. It is as if she has found a direct line to the powers up above to speak through her, to reach out to the children and teach our world of *love* and *oneness*."

—Pamela Hart, mom and founder of www.PlantTrees4Life.com

"Laura Duksta is a gift to the world and so is this book. Parents and children alike will delight in flipping the book over and over, sharing the love in *You Are a Gift to the World*. I love this book."

—Debbie Milam, author, *I Love Being Me* and founder of www.bestyoucanbe.org

"Laura Duksta has done it again! *You Are a Gift to the World* is a beautiful progression from her *New York Times* bestseller *I Love You More*. This book is itself a gift to children and the grown-ups who love them. Its message of the magnificence of our world fills my heart with hope for our world."

—Peggy McColl, *New York Times* bestselling author of *Your Destiny Switch*

"This book is as much for parents, grandparents, and teachers as it is for the children they'll share it with. What a beautiful reminder of the opportunities we are given every moment to love for no reason."

—Marci Shimoff, *New York Times* bestselling author of *Love for No Reason*, *Happy for No Reason*, and *Chicken Soup for the Woman's Soul*

"Our children are the greatest gifts to this world and sharing *You Are a Gift to the World* reminds parent and child how it's the smallest moments that capture the greatest memories and where love naturally shines brightest."

—Cynthia Litman, www.MommasPearls.com

Praise for *I Love You More*

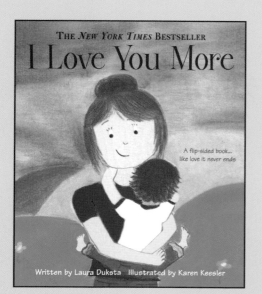

"I can just see an adult and a kid giggling away, flipping the book over and taking turns reading to get to the middle and a big fat hug…Sweet, simple examples that a little one with a big heart will understand."

—Alyne Ellis, AARP Radio Network

"I love this book because it deals with the most powerful thing in the world…love."

—Mark Victor Hansen, co-creator of the #1 *New York Times* bestselling series Chicken Soup for the Soul

"In my entire life I've never read a children's book that has touched me so deeply. *I Love You More* is simple, elegant, and moving. It's impossible for anyone to read this book without their hearts opening with tears of gratitude and love."

—Dr. John Demartini, human behavioral specialist, educator, author

"The day we received *I Love You More*, my wife read it over the phone to our youngest child. The conversation of love it sparked was magical."

—Jack Canfield, co-creator of the #1 *New York Times* bestselling series Chicken Soup for the Kid's Soul

"A great flip-story book with an appealing message!…Parents will enjoy the book's sentiments, and teachers will find it useful in the classroom. A must-have for the holidays, and a great way to say I love you!"

—Diane Van Tassell

"*I Love You More* shines as a pure expression of the heart. I wish everyone could read this book and live its glowing message."

—Alan Cohen, author of *A Deep Breath of Life*

You Are a Gift to the World

Published by Sourcebooks Jabberwocky, an imprint of Sourcebooks, Inc.
P.O. Box 4410, Naperville, Illinois 60567-4410
(630) 961-3900
Fax: (630) 961-2168
www.jabberwockykids.com

Library of Congress Cataloging-in-Publication data is on file with the publisher.

Source of Production: Leo Paper, Heshan City, Guangdong Province, China
Date of Production: January 2011
Run Number: 14149

Printed and bound in China.
LEO 10 9 8 7 6 5 4 3 2 1

I am blessed with the gifts of a magnificent family and friends.
This book is dedicated to them all and specifically to my nieces and nephews,
Michaela, Tyler, C. J., Myranda, Andrew, and Alexandra.
A big thank-you to my parents for their continued support
and to my dad for passing on his ability
to write a good poem.

Thank you, God! *I Love You More!*

I remember when you asked,
"What's the best gift in the whole wide world?"
I looked at you and knew the answer
was right inside my heart.
With a big smile I took your hand and said,
"Let's see, where shall I start?"

You are the best gift that
I have ever received.

You're a one-of-a-kind YOU
better than I could have
ever believed.

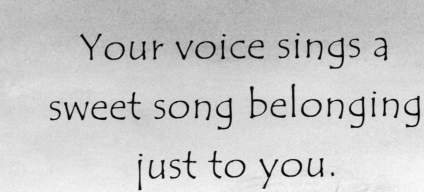

Your voice sings a
sweet song belonging
just to you.

I hear a melody filled with joy,
wonder, and a note of laughter too.

Your smile lights up my life
like the sun's golden rays.

Its glow brightens up my life
in warm and tender ways.

A big hug is the best present
you and I can share.

When you wrap your arms
around me tight, it shows
how much you care.

Your family always loves
you whether they're near
or far away.

Did you know we are all brothers and sisters in a certain special way?

You are a gift to the world and the world is a gift to you.

painting the world in colors until
you go to sleep at night.

So as you travel through life, you see all the ways it's true...

The sun shines down upon us,
a giant smile so bright;

They're Mother Nature's
pathway from the ground up
to the sky.

Can you see the snowy mountaintops,
reaching through the clouds so high?

Our oceans are a treasure chest filled with creatures big and small.

You'll find turtles, fish, and whales, and crabs that do the sideways crawl.

Flowers, plants, and trees
all start from tiny seeds.
As they grow, they help to make the
food and air your body needs.

You see the world itself is a big gift,
full of miracles just like you and me.
There is so much to discover,
to learn, to do, and to see.

I took a deep breath and let this
answer flow from my heart:
"Right here where you are standing
is the perfect place to start..."

I remember when you asked, "What's the biggest gift in the whole wide world?"

The World Is a Gift to You

A Little Bit about the Author:

Laura Duksta knew from a young age that she was meant to travel the world, meet her brothers and sisters, and spread the message of love. What she didn't know was that her life's biggest challenge, losing all her hair at age eleven to Alopecia Areata, would teach her valuable lessons about love, compassion, and understanding for humanity as well as for herself. Her first book, *New York Times* bestseller *I Love You More*, was written for her nephew Tyler and for all children so that they might know that, no matter what's going on in their lives or in the world around them, how truly loved they are. Laura believes that we are expressions of the Divine and that the love we share with each other and the world is the best and biggest gift of all. She continues to spread this message of love through her books, school programs, music, and inspirational talks.

Laura resides in Fort Lauderdale, Florida, surrounded by the love of her family and friends, cherishing the beauty and wonder of the world. For more information log onto www.LauraDuksta.com or visit her blog at www.TheConversationofLove.com.

Photo by Maggie Steber

A Little Bit about the Illustrator:

Dona Turner is an illustrator and an abstract painter. Her work, inspired by a joyful universe, uses rich texture and playful color. Dona lives in Oakland, California, with her husband Robert Mozingo, an architect and winemaker, and their little dog, ZZ-Belle. She teaches Graphic Design at the University of California, Berkeley Extension and has recently started making short documentary videos and video art installations. When she's not making art, Dona likes to wander around the world finding odd and interesting things to add to her many collections. Visit her at www.donaturner.com.

We are honored to partner with

Donating a portion of our proceeds so we can all
Keep Breathing, Keep Reading, Keep Shining!

The World Is a Gift to You

By Laura Duksta

Illustrated by Dona Turner

sourcebooks
jabberwocky

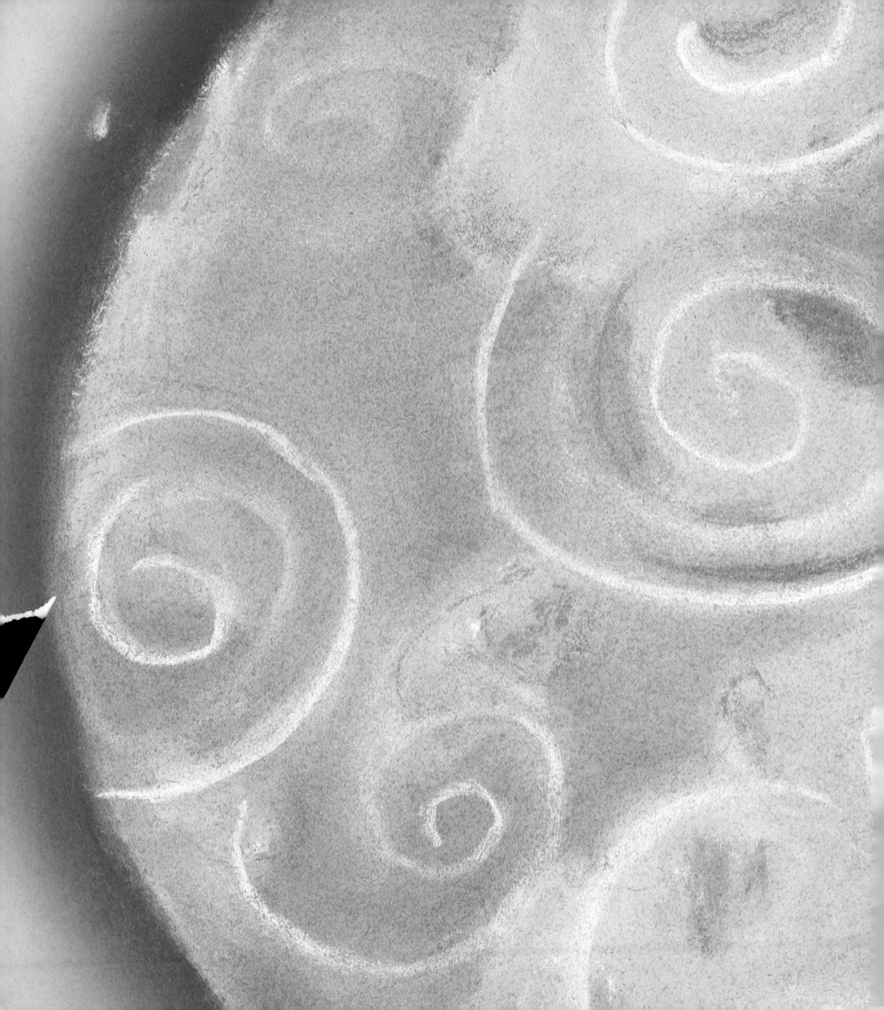